Frank Ireson

A Sketch of the Pre-Shakespearian Drama

Frank Ireson

A Sketch of the Pre-Shakespearian Drama

ISBN/EAN: 9783337394714

Printed in Europe, USA, Canada, Australia, Japan

Cover: Foto ©Andreas Hilbeck / pixelio.de

More available books at **www.hansebooks.com**

O. U.

MISCELLANIES.

No. 7.

A Sketch of the

Pre-Shakspearian Drama

BY

BRO. FRANK IRESON, B.A.Lond.

Artificer to the Sette,

Delivered at the Freemasons' Tavern, on Friday,
January 9, 1884.

Imprynted by *Bro* C. W. H. WYMAN,
Typographer to yᵉ *Sette*, at hys Printing-hovſe in Great Qveene
Street, over againſt Lincoln's Inne Fields, within yᵉ
Pariſh of Saynt Giles in yᵉ Fields
London. m.d.ccc.lxxxv.

DULCE EST DESIPERE IN LOCO.—*Horace.*

DULCE—*Delightful*, says the poet,
EST—*is it*, and right well we know it,
DESIPERE—*to play the fool*
IN LOCO—*when we're out of school.*

W. M. T.

The Pre-Shakspearian Drama.

The Pre-Shakspearian Drama.

YOUR ODDSHIP, BRETHREN, AND GUESTS.

THE paper which I have been desired to read to you this evening I have called, "A Sketch of the pre-Shakspearian Drama." In the hearing of it some of my listeners may possibly come across details not known to them : and, probably, there will be found in it much which will be familiar to many of them. In any case, I think the subject is sufficiently interesting to warrant my thus reminding you of its leading features.

The first point to be noticed in connexion with the Drama in England is, that there is no record of any attempt at acting prior to the Conquest : before that time there was a descriptive and indeed poetic literature, but it contained no trace of dramatic form. The Saxons certainly had nothing which could be termed acting ; while the Normans who came into England brought with them strolling minstrels and "jongleurs," who by song and pantomimic jest, amused all classes of the people ; but they seem to have taken no part in concerted dramatic action, and must not be regarded as having in any direct manner originated it in this country.

The prototype of English Drama is the *Miracle Play.* This consisted of a representation of Scriptural incident, enacted by the clergy for the instruction of the people. Without some such aid, in the scarcity of

books and of the ability to read them, the
masses would have had very little chance
of becoming acquainted with the essential
facts connected with the foundation and
progress of the Christian religion. The
sacred drama may be said to date as far back
as the end of the second century, when the
Early Fathers instituted it to counteract the
worldly influence of the decaying and corrupt
Roman stage : in France this combination of
dramatic action with the service of the Romish
Church seems to have been in vogue at the
time of the Conquest, and it was brought over
to England by the monks soon after that
event. These plays were first performed, in
either Latin or French, on special occasions,
or Saints' days, with the idea of bringing
home to the illiterate some leading facts of
Bible history, or some legends of the saints to
whom the churches were so freely dedicated.
The first specimen of which we have authentic
mention is the Miracle of St. Catharine,

which seems to have been played at Dun-stable about the year 1110 : all that is known about it is that it was acted at the instigation of a certain Geoffrey of Gorham, and that he borrowed copes from St. Albans for the decoration of it. For a good example of a miracle play we may take one by Hilarius, written in France in the time of Stephen, or perhaps a little later.

"In a church dedicated to St. Nicholas, upon St. Nicholas Day, the image of the Saint was removed, and a living actor, dressed to represent the statue, was placed in the shrine. When the pause was made in the service for the acting of the Miracle, one came in at the church-door dressed as a rich heathen, deposited his treasure at the shrine, said that he was going on a journey, and called on the Saint to be the guardian of his property. When the heathen had gone out, thieves entered and silently carried off the treasure. Then came the heathen back and furiously raged : he took a whip and began to thrash the image of the Saint. But upon this the image moved, descended from its niche, went out, and reasoned with the robbers, threatening also to denounce them to the people. Terrified by this miracle, the thieves returned tremblingly, and so in silence they brought everything back. The statue was again in its niche, motionless. The heathen sang his joy to a popular tune of the time, and turned to adore the image. Then St. Nicholas himself appeared, bidding the heathen worship God alone and praise the name of Christ. The heathen was converted. The piece ended with the adoration of the Almighty, and the Church service was then continued."

Besides these representations of miracles worked by the Saints, there were also " Mysteries," which portrayed, in similar fashion, the incidents connected with the birth, passion, and resurrection of Christ.

The title of "Mystery" was borrowed from France, but it does not seem to have been used in England, where representations of this class were always known as "Miracle Plays." The dialogue of these productions was, for the most part, extremely rude and ·inartificial, and they cannot be said to have had any regular plot: they were really a series of shows or pageants, being indeed called by the latter name. They were generally exhibited during the Christmas and Easter holidays, and were frequently got up and acted by the trading companies in the larger cities, each guild undertaking a portion of the performance, and sustaining a share of the expense. At both Coventry and Chester these plays were exhibited with a considerable amount of elaborateness, and the MSS. used in these two places are still in existence. A third series remains to us, that in the Townley collection: the latter dates from the fourteenth century ; there are thirty-two plays in it, and they comprehensively range from the Creation to Doomsday! It is worthy of notice that the London trading companies seem to have taken no part in work of this character.

When first introduced, the play was merely a part of the Church service, and was performed by the clergy only. In course of time the interest in these productions increased, and they were transferred to a series of scaffolds erected at the door of the church, the audience being outside in the street or churchyard. From the scaffold so fixed to a locomotive stage the transition would be easy, and it seems probable that with this change the acting would, to some extent, pass from the clergy to that of laymen. A class of itinerant actors thus came into existence, who wheeled their stage into various towns, and played before the people both in front of the church and in the open streets. It seems likely that about this time the English language was introduced into the representations, instead of the original Latin or French.

A common addition to the rude attempts at scenery was the representation of Hell at a lower level than the stage : this generally took the form of a whale's mouth, a very ancient way of indicating the entrance to the Infernal Regions, out of which flame and smoke were caused to emerge : in one place we read of a man being paid 3d. for "keeping up Hell fire." The Devil naturally was a prominent personage employed, and he seems to have frequently represented the comic and noisy element in the play : his roarings and ragings must have contributed not a little to the amusement of an uneducated crowd, whose chief idea of humour would be found in boisterous buffoonery.

At first, and especially when acted in church, these plays consisted entirely of Scriptural and legendary incidents, but gradually they developed the latent passion for acting for its own sake, the result being that the sacred subject was constantly overlaid with a great deal that was decidedly profane. The proclamation of the Chester plays, for instance, expressly excuses the introduction of " some things not warranted by any writ," on the ground that it was done to " make sport " and to " glad the hearers." The clergy seem to have taken a great amount of interest in the mounting and acting of these plays, and to have entered with great zest into their production ; so far did they carry their passion for taking part in them, the which was by no means prohibited by their clerical vocation, that the bishops were occasionally constrained to moderate the vigour of their enthusiasm. The following excerpt from a tract printed in the early part of Elizabeth's reign shows how the clergy would at times neglect their duties : " He again posteth over it [the service] as fast as he can gallop : for either he hath two places to serve, or else

there are some games to be played in the after-
noon, as lying for the whetstone, heathenishe
dauncing for a ring, a beare or a bull to be
bayted, or else jack-an-apes to ride on horse-
back, or an enterlude to be played : and if
no place else can be gotten, it must be done
in the church ! "

These Miracle Plays were in vogue shortly
after the Conquest, and continued to be
popular until about the end of Elizabeth's
reign, the last one being acted at Kendal in
the reign of James I.: they were, previously
to the introduction of printing, one of the
principal means of teaching the people, and,
after their fashion, seemed to have done good
service to that end. We may here parenthe-
tically recall the fact, that in England the
women's parts were always impersonated by
boys down to the time of Charles II.; during
the reign of that lively monarch women
appeared for the first time upon the stage,
much to the disgust of the Puritans, though

for some time previously their employment as actresses had been common in Spain, Italy, and France.

We have already seen that after a time there were introduced into these Miracle Plays various representations and characters not specifically referred to either in Scripture history or saintly legend : this was probably done partly for the sake of variety, many comic characters being introduced to amuse the people, and partly because it was found that a much better and more forcible portrayal of Biblical history was rendered possible by the introduction of allegorical characters. As the presentation of these Miracle Plays became common, we find that there were gradually introduced into them impersona-tions of many of the virtues and vices, thus lending reality to the show, and giving visible reason for much of the action which took place. It was in this way that the *Moral Plays* came into existence. They may be defined as plays designed to illustrate and enforce some moral precept, to which end there were introduced into them allegorical figures, who personated various passions, virtues, and sins commonly to be met with. These characters, as they became more numerous, interfered to a certain degree with the progress of the action : so much so that in some pieces the Scriptural characters fell quite into the background ; and thus, in course of time, what seems to have been at first designed as a kind of poetical embellishment to an historical drama became a new species of drama unconnected with history. These Moral Plays were in a considerable state of advancement early in the reign of Henry VI., and they appear to have existed side by side with the Miracle Plays until both were gradually extinguished by the regular drama,—their life ending at about the date of the death of Shakspeare.   Both these forms of entertainment seldom lasted over an hour in performance, and of those which were in two parts each part was exhibited on a separate day.

Besides allegorical personages, there were two standing characters very prominent in Moral Plays,—the Devil and Vice. The Devil was, no doubt, introduced from the Miracle Plays, where he had figured so amusingly : he was made as hideous as possible by his mask and dress, the latter being generally of a shaggy and hairy character, and he was duly provided with a tail : his ordinary exclamation on entering was, " Ho, ho, ho ! what a felowe am I ! " and he was much given to roaring and crying out, especially when he was belaboured by his constant companion, Vice. The latter had various names, according to the sin which he represented, and appeared in many disguises : one of his most frequent costumes was that of the common fool, and he seems to have constantly misconducted himself to even a greater extent than did the Devil, who generally wound up his career by taking him upon his back and running off with him to Hell. He occasionally appeared by himself as an independent character. In the " Life and Repentance of Mary Magdalene " we find him performing the part of her lover, and recommending her not to make " two hells instead of one," but to live merrily in this world, since she is sure to be damned in the next. The later Moral Plays were written quite independently of Scriptural or saintly associations : one of them, produced during the reign of Elizabeth, was wholly *political* in its design. It is interesting as being one of the earliest productions in which the stage was employed as a vehicle for satirising and denouncing the political abuses of the day.

So much for the Miracle and Moral Plays, which, as has been stated, died out at the end of the reign of Elizabeth : a modified form of them, known as Pageants or Masks, and consisting of processions of various kinds existed for nearly a century later, and was then incorporated with the regular drama. Readers of Walter Scott's " Kenilworth " will remember that the Pageant and Mask were popular forms of entertainment in the time of Elizabeth, the former being of a purely spectacular character. While the latter may be said to have occupied an intermediate space between Pageant and Play.

The connecting link between the Moral Plays and the Drama proper is to be found in the *Interludes*, which came into fashion in the time of Henry VIII., and were gradually developed into fuller form during the sixteenth century. John Heywood, a musician of Henry's household, set the first example of composing interludes quite independently of allegorical materials; some of his " mery plays " were distinctly comic, and their prescribed action nothing less than farcical.

We may pause for a moment to observe

the extraordinary manner in which, in the middle of the sixteenth century, " our drama and our dramatic literature rose," as a well-known writer puts it, " with all but unequalled swiftness to the highest perfection to which they have attained." For some five hundred years the only dramatic art in England was to be found in the Miracle and Moral Plays, which were slowly developed in extent and dialogue, as the people gradually acquired intelligence and some interest in things refined. Then during the half-century of the reign of Elizabeth we find an advance in both dramatic and literary art, which is rightly deemed marvellous. This was due to various causes, amongst which may be named the more extended introduction of printing, the cultivation of classical studies in the universities and schools, and the general increase in the political tranquillity and material prosperity of the people. Account for it as we will, the fact remains that during the Elizabethan period the English Drama made a great stride from comparative infancy to a maturity which has certainly never been surpassed in the history of our dramatic literature, and with which the name of Shakspeare must be inseparably connected.

To complete our sketch of the pre-Shakspearian drama it now remains to mention the earliest plays extant, which may be considered to have originated the various styles used for these productions, and the principal authors concerned in its foundation and early advancement. It may here be observed that the term "Comedy," was, during this period, much more inclusive in its meaning than in modern times : it was synonymous, in fact, with our word "Play." Hamlet, it will be remembered, after he has had the tragedy exhibited before the king and queen, exclaims,—

"For if the king like not the comedy," &c. The term "Tragedy," on the other hand, pertained not only to plays of a tragic nature, but to any serious narrative in verse.

In the earliest specimen of English Comedy which has come down to us we have also the first avowed dramatic imitation in English of the ancients. This was " Ralph Roister Doister," which was probably written before the beginning of Elizabeth's reign : the author was Nicholas Udall, who was a master first at Eton, and then at Westminster school. It was written for the Eton boys to perform, and was admittedly a copy, as far as concerns style, of Plautus and Terence. It was divided into acts and scenes, and had nine male and four female characters, its time of performance being two hours. Another comedy of about the same date, named " Misogonus," had its scene laid in Italy, and was evidently adapted from some Italian play. A third early comedy was " Gammer Gurton's Needle," written by Still, afterwards Bishop of Bath and Wells ; this was acted at Cambridge in

1566, and is remarkable as the first existing English play that was acted at either University.

The earliest piece which can properly be termed a tragedy was written by Thomas Sackville (afterwards Earl of Dorcet), and Thos. Norton, a barrister : it was acted before the Queen at Whitehall in 1561. It bears two names, " The Tragedy of Gorboduc," or, more correctly, " The Tragedy of Ferrex and Porrex," and its plot is based upon an old British legend : this production is noticeable as being the first English play written in blank verse. The tragedy of " Julius Cæsar," which followed soon after it, is the earliest instance on record of English dramatisation of Roman history.

At about this time the dramatic field would seem to have been about equally divided between the later Moral Plays and the earlier " Comedies, tragedies, interludes, and stage plays," as a print of the time has it ; soon, however, the former became confined to country places, and ultimately died out altogether.

The immediate predecessors of Shakspeare did their part in improving the drama, and two of them may be named as having done good work to this end,—Lyly and Marlowe. The former was the originator of that fantastic style of writing and speaking known as Euphuism, which became so fashionable in his time: the latter, Christopher Marlowe, was a writer of considerable power, who has been termed, and not unjustly, the father of English dramatic poetry: this title has been given to him in consideration of the excellent service which he did in refining and generally improving the standard of play-writing in his day—he may be said to have prepared the way for his great successor, by his influence on the public taste and appreciative power.

Of the younger contemporaries of

Shakspeare it will be sufficient here to mention Ben Jonson, Beaumont, Fletcher, Massinger, Shirley, and Ford. A criticism of their work would exceed the limits of this paper.

To recapitulate : it has been shown that the Drama in England had its origin in religious worship ; and that some five centuries elapsed between its introduction by monkish hands in a tongue " not understanded of the people," and its full and popular development under the prolific and versatile genius of Shakspeare. Its emancipation as a form of art,—and especially in conjunction with literature,—progressed but slowly during the greater part of this period : at the end of that time, however, its advance towards maturity became most thorough and rapid. The termination of the Elizabethan age marks an epoch in history which will be looked back upon with interest and admiration so long as the English language shall exist, and the

period is one at which may fittingly be ter-
minated this short and necessarily slight
sketch of the origin and early development
of the English Drama.

O. V.

A

BIBLIOGRAPHY

OF THE

PRIVATELY PRINTED OPUSCULA

Issued to the Members of the Sette of Odd Volumes,

Imprynted by *Bro* C. W. H. WYMAN,

Typographer vnto yᵉ *Sette*, at hys Printinge-hovſe in Great Qveene Street, over agaynſt Lincoln's Inne Fields, wythin yᵉ Paryſhe of Saynt Giles in yᵉ Fields in *Londonne.*

"Books that can be held in the hand, and carried to the fireside, are the best after all."—*Samuel Johnson.*

"The writings of the wise are the only riches our posterity cannot squander."—*Charles Lamb.*

I.   ## B. Q.

A Biographical and Bibliographical Fragment. 22 Pages. Presented on November the 5th, 1880, by His Oddship C. W. H. WYMAN.   1st Edition limited to 25 copies.
(Subsequently enlarged to 50 copies.)

II.   ## Glossographia Anglicana.

By the late J. TROTTER BROCKETT, F.S.A., London and Newcastle, author of "Glossary of North Country Words," to which is prefixed a Biographical Sketch of the Author by FREDERICK BLOOMER. 94 Pages. Presented on July the 7th, 1882, by His Oddship BERNARD QUARITCH.

Edition limited to 150 copies.

III. Ye Boke of Ye Odd Volumes

from 1878 to 1883. Carefvlly *Compiled* and painsfvlly *Edited* by ye vnworthy *Historiographer* to ye Sette, *Brother* and *Vice-President* WILLIAM MORT THOMPSON, and produced by ye order and at ye charges of Hys Oddship ye President and Librarian of ye Sette, Bro. BERNARD QUARITCH. (pp. 136.) Presented on April the 13th, 1883, by His Oddship BERNARD QUARITCH.

Edition limited to 150 copies.

IV. Lobes Garland ;

Or Posies for Rings, Hand-kerchers, & Gloves, and such pretty Tokens that Lovers send their Loves. London, 1674. A Reprint. And Ye Garland of Ye Odd Volumes. (pp. 102.) Presented on October the 12th, 1883, by Bro. JAMES ROBERTS BROWN.   Edition limited to 250 copies.

V. Queen Anne Musick.

A brief Accompt of ye genuine Article, those who performed ye same, and ye Masters in ye facultie.   From 1702 to 1714.   (pp. 40.)   Presented on July the 13th, 1883, by Bro. BURNHAM W. HORNER.

Edition limited to 100 copies.

VI. A Very Odd Dream.

Related by His Oddship Bro. W. M. THOMPSON, President of the Sette of Odd Volumes, at the Freemasons' Tavern, Great Queen Street, on June 1st, 1883. (pp. 26.) Presented on July the 13th, 1883, by His Oddship W. MORT THOMPSON.   Edition limited to 250 copies.

VII. Codex Chiromantiae.

Being a Compleate Manualle of ye Science and Arte of Expoundynge ye Past, ye Presente, ye Future, and ye Charactere, by ye Scrutinie of ye Hande, ye Gestures thereof, and ye Chirographie. *Codicillus I.*—CHIROGNOMY (pp. 118.) Presented on November the 2nd, by Bro. ED. HERON-ALLEN.   Edition limited to 133 copies.

VIII. **Intaglio Engraving: Past and Present.**

An Address by Bro. EDWARD RENTON, delivered at the Freemasons' Tavern, Great Queen Street, on December 5, 1884. (pp. 74.) Presented to the Sette by His Oddship EDWARD F. WYMAN. Edition limited to 200 copies.

MISCELLANIES.

I. **Inaugural Address**

of His Oddship, W. M. THOMPSON, Fourth President of the Sette of Odd Volumes, delivered at the Freemasons' Tavern, Great Queen Street, on his taking office on April 13th, 1883, &c. (pp. 31.) Printed by order of Ye Sette, and issued on May the 4th, 1883.
Edition limited to 250 copies.

II. **Codex Chiromantiae.**

Appendix A. Dactylomancy, or Finger-ring Magic, Ancient, Mediæval, and Modern. (pp. 34.) Presented on October the 12th, 1883, by Bro. ED. HERON-ALLEN.
Edition limited to 133 copies.

III. **A President's Persiflage.**

Spoken by His Oddship W. M. THOMPSON, Fourth President of the Sette of Odd Volumes, at the Freemasons' Tavern, Great Queen Street, at the Fifty-eighth Meeting of the Sette, on December 7th, 1883. (pp. 15.)
Edition limited to 250 copies.

IV. **Inaugural Address**

of His Oddship EDWARD F. WYMAN, Fifth President of the Sette of Odd Volumes, delivered at the Freemasons' Tavern, Great Queen Street, on his taking office, on April 4th, 1884, &c. (pp. 56.) Presented to the Sette by His Oddship EDWARD F. WYMAN.
Edition limited to 133 copies.

C

"There is Divinity in Odd Numbers."—*Shakespeare.*

Ye Sette of Ye Odd Volumes.

April 4, 1884.

✠:✠:✠:✠:✠:✠:✠:✠:✠

EDWARD HERON ALLEN, *Necromancer,*
St. John's, Putney Hill, S.W.

JAMES ROBERTS BROWN, *Alchymist*
(*Secretary,* 1880; *Vice-President,* 1883),
14, Hilldrop Road, Tufnell Park, N.

GEORGE CLULOW, *Xylographer*
(*Secretary,* 1881), VICE-PRESIDENT,
51, Belsize Avenue, Hampstead, N.W.

ALFRED J. DAVIES, *Attorney-General*
(*Vice-President,* 1881), SECRETARY,
21, Churchfield Road, Mattock Lane, Ealing, W.

CHARLES LEOPOLD EBERHARDT, *Astrologer,*
Thuringia House, Fitzjohn Avenue, Hampstead, N.W.

GEORGE CHARLES HAITÉ, *Art Critic,*
Ormsby Lodge, Blandford Road, Bedford Park, W.

BURNHAM W. HORNER, *Organist,*
34, Sheen Park, Richmond, S.W.

FRANK IRESON, *Artificer,*
81, Caversham Road, N.W.

EDWARD LANG, *Armourer*,
89, Wigmore Street, W.

HENRY GEORGE LILEY, *Art Director*,
Radnor House, Radnor Place, Gloucester Square,
Hyde Park, W.

WILLIAM MURRELL, M.D., *Leech*
(*Secretary*, 1883),
38, Weymouth Street, Portland Place, W.

BERNARD QUARITCH, *Librarian*
(*President*, 1878, 1879, & 1882),
15, Piccadilly, W.

EDWARD RENTON, *Herald*
(*Vice-President*, 1880 ; *Secretary*, 1882)
44, South Hill Park, Hampstead, N.W.

H. J. GORDON ROSS, *Master of Ceremonies*,
Hillrise, Putney Hill, S.W.

W. M. THOMPSON, *Historiographer*
(*Vice-President*, 1882 ; *President*, 1883),
16, Carlyle Square, Chelsea, S.W.

G. R. TYLER, *Stationer*,
127, Tulse Hill, S.W.

T. C. VENABLES, *Antiquary*,
17, Queenhithe, E.C.

CORNELIUS WALFORD, *Master of the Rolls*,
Enfield House, Belsize Park Gardens, N.W.

CHARLES W. H. WYMAN, *Typographer*
(*Vice-President*, 1878 & 1879 ; *President*, 1880),
103, King Henry's Road, Primrose Hill, N.W.

EDWARD F. WYMAN, *Treasurer*
(*Secretary*, 1878 & 1879), PRESIDENT,
11, Endsleigh Street, Tavistock Square W.C.

J. B. ZERBINI, *Musical Referee*,
7. Rochester Villas, Camden Road, N.W.

Supplemental Odd Volumes.

WILFRED BALL, *Peintre-Graveur*,
39B, Old Bond Street, W.

DANIEL W. KETTLE, F.R.G.S., *Cosmographer*,
Hayes Common, near Beckenham, Kent.

CHARLES WELSH, *Chapman*,
2, Ludgate Hill, E.C.

Foreign Corresponding Members.

J. H. UPTON, Esq.,
Auckland, New Zealand.

WILLIAM MATTHEWS, Esq.,
Irving Place, Flatbush, Long Island, U.S.A.